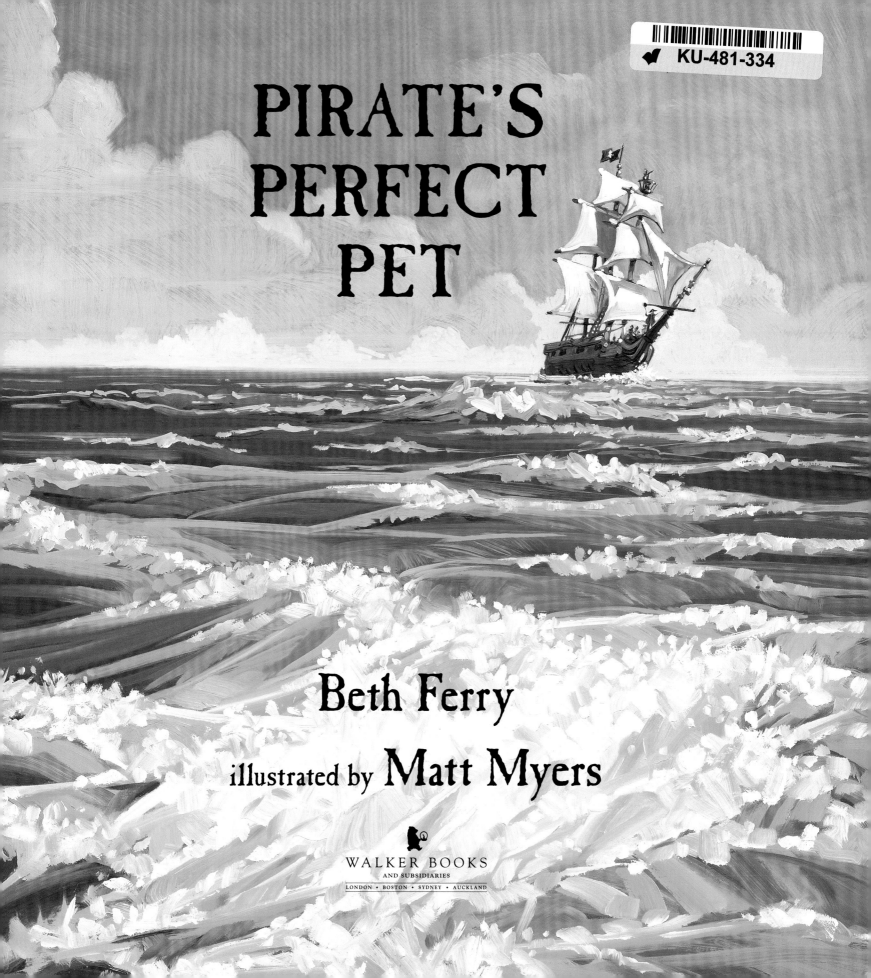

PIRATE'S PERFECT PET

Beth Ferry

illustrated by Matt Myers

WALKER BOOKS
AND SUBSIDIARIES

LONDON • BOSTON • SYDNEY • AUCKLAND

PIRATE'S PERFECT PET

THAR BE→
AUDITIONS

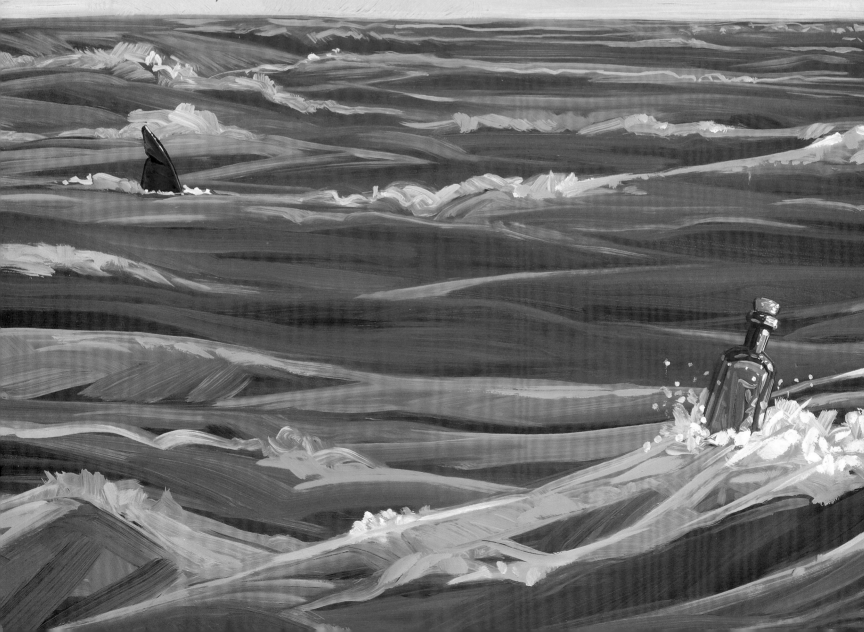

FOR ME MUM
B. F.

FOR ME FIRST MATE, MAYA
M. M.

First published 2016 by Walker Books Ltd, 87 Vauxhall Walk, London SE11 5HJ · Text © 2016 Beth Ferry · Illustrations © 2016 Matt Myers · The right of Beth Ferry and Matt Myers to be identif[...] as author and illustrator respectively of this work has been asserted by them in accordance with the Copyright, Designs and Patents Act 1988 · This book has been typeset in Caslon Antiq[...] Printed in China · All rights reserved. No part of this book may be reproduced, transmitted or stored in an information retrieval system in any form or by any means, graphic, electronic [...] mechanical, including photocopying, taping and recording, without prior written permission from the publisher. · British Library Cataloguing in Publication Data: a catalogue record for th[...] book is available from the British Library · ISBN 978-1-4063-7110-9 · www.walker.co.uk · 10 9 8 7 6 5 4 3 2 1

From the deck of his pirate ship, the *Sea Dragon*,
Captain Crave spied a small blue bottle bobbing
among the waves ... and the sharks.
Captain Crave was courageous.
He was daring.
He was ...

gone.

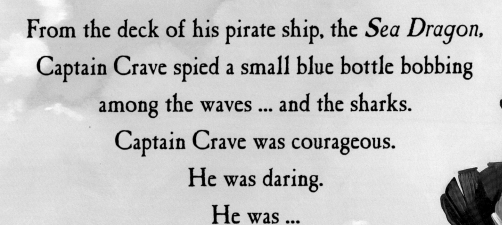

With a flawless dive, he sliced through the water
and snagged the cork with his hook.

His crew cheered
and waved and chanted,
"Go, Crave!"
and caused quite a commotion,
as good pirates should.

After taking a bow, Captain Crave
uncorked the treasure within.

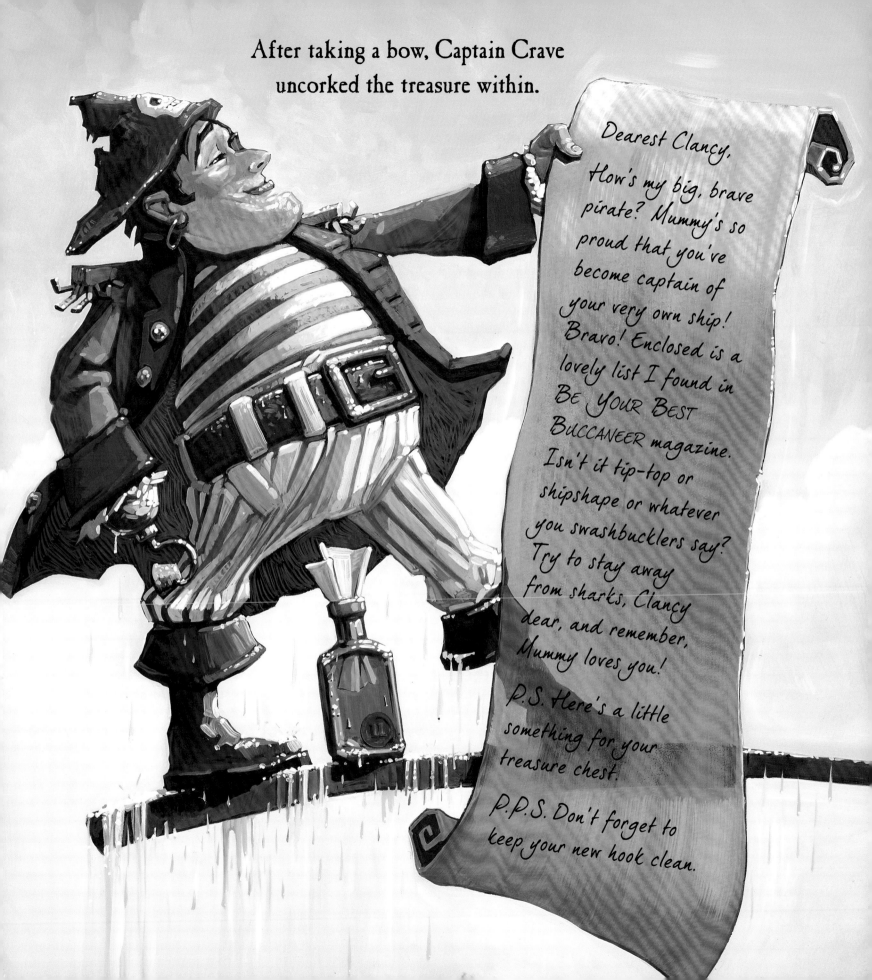

Dearest Clancy,

How's my big, brave pirate? Mummy's so proud that you've become captain of your very own ship! Bravo! Enclosed is a lovely list I found in BE YOUR BEST BUCCANEER magazine. Isn't it tip-top or shipshape or whatever you swashbucklers say? Try to stay away from sharks, Clancy dear, and remember, Mummy loves you!

P.S. Here's a little something for your treasure chest.

P.P.S. Don't forget to keep your new hook clean.

Captain Crave stuffed the letter
and the shiny doubloon into his pocket.
"Me mum," he said with a shrug,
handing the list to his first mate.

"Think you're the Perfect Pirate Captain?" she read.
"Use our handy checklist to be sure.
Ship?"

"Check," replied the captain.

"That's what it says."

"Well, shuck me an oyster
and set sail for land.
We needs to find me a pet."

The pirates anchored on a sandy beach.
They caused quite a commotion, as good pirates should.

They set about at once scooping and digging.

"Crab?"

"Too cranky."

"Octopus?"

"Too clingy."

"Clam?"

"Too quiet."

"Drat," said Captain Crave.

"Thar be no perfect pets on the beach. Onward ho."

The pirates marched onward until they came to a farm.
They caused quite a commotion, as good pirates should.

The crew scurried about, grabbing and herding.

"*Goat?*"

"Too nibbly."

"*Pig?*"

"Too muddy."

"*Donkey?*"

"Too stubborn."

"Goose?"

"Too bossy."

"Drat," said Captain Crave.

"Thar be no perfect pets on the farm. Onward ho."

The pirates marched onward until they came to a zoo.
They caused quite a commotion, as good pirates should.

The crew began unlocking and unleashing.

"Elephant?"

"Too big."

"Koala?"

"Too cuddly."

"Lion?"

"Yikes!"

When the uproar finally died down, Captain Crave said,
"Well, I've finally got me peg leg!"

"Check," scribbled the first mate.

"Now if I could only find me a pet."

The harried zookeeper stuffed the pirates into a trolley and drove directly to ...

the Pet Emporium.

The pirates crowded eagerly into the shop.
There were kittens and bunnies, guppies and puppies –
all kinds of cute, cuddly creatures.

"Shiver me Shih Tzus," Captain Crave exclaimed.
"Thar be piles of pets!"

Just then there was a
squawk from above.

The captain looked up.
SPLAT!

"I've been poop-decked,"
he yelled.

e pirates chased the birdie.

They raced the birdie.

"Should we taste the birdie?"

"Give 'er here," ordered the captain.
He eyed the parrot closely. "Ahhh," he murmured.

"Yer a brave one, I see."
    "Aye," said the parrot.

"Ye pooped in me eye."
    "Eye," echoed the parrot.

"And caused quite a commotion."
    "Aye," agreed the parrot.

"Like a good parrot should."
    "Aye?" asked the parrot.

"And everything would be perfect," the captain mused,
"if I could only find me a pet. Do ye happen to know –
in land, sea, or sky – any pirate-worthy pets?"

The parrot stepped onto Captain Crave's shoulder and nibbled his ear.
"I," said the parrot.

ONWARD HO!

Captain Crave flipped his shiny doubloon to the shopkeeper
as he thumped out the door,
the perfect pirate captain with the perfect parrot pet.